Classic Adventures

Treasure Island

by
Robert Louis Stevenson

retold by
John Matern

Don Johnston Incorporated
Volo, Illinois

Edited by:

Jerry Stemach, MS, CCC-SLP

Gail Portnuff Venable, MS, CCC-SLP

Dorothy Tyack, MA

Consultant:

Ted S. Hasselbring, PhD

Graphics and Illustrations:

Photographs and illustrations are all created professionally and modified to provide the best possible support for the intended reader.

Narration:

Professional actors and actresses read the text to build excitement and to model research-based elements of fluency: intonation, stress, prosody, phrase groupings and rate. The rate has been set to maximize comprehension for the reader.

Published by:

Don Johnston Incorporated
26799 West Commerce Drive
Volo, IL 60073

800.999.4660 USA Canada
800.889.5242 Technical Support
www.donjohnston.com

DON JOHNSTON

International Standard Book Number
ISBN-10: 1-893376-03-6
ISBN-13: 978-1-893376-03-8

Contents

Chapter 1
The Pirate's Sea Chest **1**

Chapter 2
The Dead Man's Secret **12**

Chapter 3
Going Out to Sea **26**

Chapter 4
We Declare War **38**

Chapter 5
The Fighting Begins **51**

Chapter 6
Fighting at the Fort **63**

Chapter 7
My Trip on the Raft **73**

Chapter 8
Me and Hands **83**

Chapter 9
The Enemy Camp **97**

Chapter 10
The Treasure **109**

About the Start-to-Finish® Author **123**
About the Original Author **124**

Chapter 1

The Pirate's Sea Chest

My name is Jim Hawkins. My friends asked me to write down the story of Treasure Island from the beginning to the end. My friends do not want me to leave anything out. But there is one thing that I cannot tell you. I cannot tell you where Treasure Island is because there is still treasure on Treasure Island.

I remember the story well. It all started when an old pirate came to stay at my father's inn. The pirate's name was Captain Bill Flint.

Flint was a tall, strong man with brown skin and long hair. His hands were big and rough. They had bad cuts and scars all over them. Flint also had a long scar on his face that went from his ear to his chin. His clothes were dirty and old. He owned a big wooden chest. The chest was so heavy that Flint could not lift it. He had to drag it behind him.

Captain Bill Flint decided to stay at my father's inn. Flint said that he would pay us for the room later.

"Fifteen men on the dead man's chest, Yo-ho-ho, and a bottle of rum!"

We were all too scared to ask him to pay us right away. My father was very sick and my mother was taking care of him. So I saw Captain Flint the most. In the daytime, Captain Flint was a quiet man. He did not talk to anyone. When someone asked him a question, he would not answer. But at night, Captain Flint was different. He would drink a lot of rum, get drunk, and then start to sing this song:

"Fifteen men on the dead man's chest, Yo-ho-ho, and a bottle of rum!"

Captain Flint seemed nervous. He was always looking out of the windows. He even paid me to look, too. He told me to look out for a pirate with one leg. Flint was afraid of this pirate. I never did see the pirate with one leg. But other pirates did come to see Captain Flint.

One pirate's name was Black Dog. He did not look at all like Captain Flint. Black Dog was a small man and he wore clean clothes. Two of Black Dog's fingers had been cut off.

I went to see what happened, and I saw Black Dog running from the inn.

Captain Flint was not happy to see Black Dog. The two pirates talked for a long time. Then I heard a scream. I went to see what happened, and I saw Black Dog running from the inn. Black Dog was bleeding from his back.

After Black Dog's visit, Captain Flint drank more and more rum. He drank so much rum that he could not even get out of bed.

Another pirate came to the inn and found Captain Flint in bed. This pirate's name was Pew. Pew was blind.

Another pirate came to the inn and found Captain
Flint in bed.

He was the dirtiest man that I have
ever seen. Pew's clothes were like
a bunch of rags, and he had a bad
smell. He did not say anything to
Captain Flint. Pew just put a piece
of paper in Flint's hand. The paper
had a black spot on it and the words
'TEN O'CLOCK.'

Flint looked at the paper. Then he
said to me, "That's it for me, Jim.
Some pirates will be coming here to
kill me at 10 o'clock tonight."

Flint took another drink of rum and pointed to his old, beat-up chest. "That's what they want."

I looked at the chest. Then I looked at Flint. He was still pointing at the chest. His hand seemed to be stuck in the air. His body jumped a little and then stopped. He fell to the floor. Captain Bill Flint was dead.

Chapter 2

The Dead Man's Secret

When I saw Captain Flint die, I cried.
I did not like him at all, but I still felt
sad. I was thinking about my father.
He was going to die soon, too.
I went downstairs. My mother heard
me crying, and she came to see me.
I told her the whole story. I told her
how pirates were coming at 10 o'clock
to kill Captain Flint. But now Captain
Flint was already dead! I told her that
the pirates wanted something in
Captain Flint's chest.

Captain Flint never paid us for
staying at our inn.

My mother really needed the money that he owed us. My mother did not think that the pirates who wanted to kill Captain Flint would want to pay his bill, too. So my mother and I decided to look in Flint's chest. There might be money there. But we had to hurry. It was already dark out and those pirates would be coming soon!

We went upstairs and slowly opened the door of Flint's room. I held up a candle and looked in.

The candle light made long shadows.
I looked on the floor at the dead body.

My mother tapped me on the
shoulder. I jumped! "We need the
key for the chest," she said. "Look in
his pockets." I crept over to the body
and put my hand into each pocket.
No key. Then I saw it. The key was on
a string, and the string was around the
dead captain's neck! I slowly lifted the
string. I was shaking. I handed the
key to my mother, but I kept looking at
Flint.

My mother opened the lock and
lifted the lid of the chest. I held up
the candle so that we could see
inside the chest. The first thing that
we saw was a new shirt that had never
been worn. Under the shirt were
three sticks of tobacco, two pistols,
some seashells, and a bar of silver.
But under all that, there were two
more things: a bag of gold and a box
of papers.

My mother only wanted what Captain
Flint owed us. She counted the gold
coins slowly.

Mother and I hid by the side of the inn and waited.

She wanted to make sure that she did not take too much. But before she could finish, we heard the pirates coming! My mother took the coins that she had, and I grabbed the box of papers. We left the candle in the room. It was very dark now and we had to feel our way down the stairs. Just as we snuck out the back door, the pirates came in the front door.

Mother and I hid by the side of the inn and waited. We saw that Pew, the blind pirate, was waiting outside in front of the inn.

When the other pirates found Captain Flint, one of them yelled out the window, "Bill is dead!"

Pew yelled back, "Well, that's less work for us. Just get the chest!"

The other pirates yelled back, "Somebody's already been here! The chest is open and the map is gone!"

Pew yelled back, "It's that boy! Find the boy!"

Pew, who was blind, ran right into the doctor's horse.

Just then, Doctor Livesey rode up
to the inn on his horse. The doctor
was taking care of my sick father and
had come to visit him. Doctor Livesey
saw the pirates, took out his gun,
and shot at them. The pirates ran in
all directions. Pew, who was blind,
ran right into the doctor's horse.
The horse jumped and stepped on
Pew. Pew fell and lay dead on the
ground. The other pirates ran away.

I told Doctor Livesey about the gold
and the box of papers from the chest.

The doctor said that we should
show these things to his friend,
Squire John.

The squire was a rich man who
lived in a big house. It was late at
night when the doctor and I rode
up to the squire's house.

A servant opened the front door
and led us to a large room that was
filled with books. Squire John was
sitting in a chair by a fire.
The doctor told the squire about
the pirates, the gold, and the box
of papers.

It was the map to Treasure Island.

The squire looked excited.

The doctor put the box on a table.

He carefully unfolded the papers.

Suddenly, a map fell out! It was
the map to Treasure Island.

The map showed that Captain Flint
had buried more than a million
dollars worth of gold on Treasure
Island! And now we knew where
to find it!

The next day Squire John said
that he wanted to buy the best
sailing ship in all of England.

We were excited about sailing to Treasure Island. But Doctor Livesey was worried. "Someone else wants that gold, too," he said.

"Who?" asked the squire.

"The pirates!" said the doctor.

Chapter 3

Going Out to Sea

Two weeks later, Squire John wrote me a letter. In the letter, the squire said that he found a beautiful ship. The ship was called the 'Hispaniola.' And the squire also said that he met a wonderful sailor who was called Long John Silver. Silver had only one leg. He was a good cook. He knew all the best sailors. Silver and the squire hired these other sailors to sail the ship for us. The squire wanted me to come and meet the whole crew. The squire also wanted his three servants to come, too.

When we got there, the squire sent me to meet Long John Silver, the cook with one leg. I was afraid to meet him because Captain Flint had warned me about a pirate with one leg. But I was happy when I saw Silver. I thought that he was the kindest man I had ever met. He ran a little tavern called the Spy Glass. Silver was friendly, and all of the men in the tavern liked him a lot. He was happy to meet me, too. His left leg was cut off at his hip.

Silver and I walked along the dock to see our new ship.

Silver used a crutch, and he could hop around quickly. He had a pet parrot that sat on his shoulder. I knew that Long John Silver and I would be great friends.

Silver and I walked along the dock to see our new ship. As we passed other ships, Silver told me all about them. I began to learn words like 'cargo' and 'rigging.' At last we came to the Hispaniola, and I met the captain of the crew. His name was Captain Smollett.

The captain was talking with Squire John and Doctor Livesey.

Captain Smollett was not happy. He was yelling at the squire. "I don't like this trip at all!"

The doctor spoke to the captain. "Why don't you like this trip?" he asked.

The captain answered, "I don't like it because I did not choose these men to sail with me. I don't know if I can trust them.

He said, "If you are looking for treasure, then you keep that a secret.

And besides that, I don't like looking for treasure! People get killed looking for treasure."

The squire was getting angry, too. He yelled back at the captain. "Long John Silver chose these men, and Silver has been sailing all of his life."

But the captain was not finished. He said, "If you are looking for treasure, then you keep that a secret. The whole darn crew knows about the treasure. Even the parrot knows about it!"

Doctor Livesey looked at Squire John. The captain was right. The squire had told the crew about the treasure. "Well," said the doctor. "From now on we will keep the treasure map a secret."

The captain was still not happy, but he agreed to go on the trip. Then he put me to work. "On my ship, everyone works," he said.

We started the trip the next day. The Hispaniola was the best of ships, and the trip went well.

I spent all my free time with Long John Silver and his parrot.

Silver said that his parrot was 200 years old! The parrot's name was Flint. Long John knew Captain Bill Flint and gave Flint's name to the parrot. I thought about Captain Flint again. I still did not like him.

Flint the parrot loved to talk. It said things like, "Pieces of eight! Pieces of eight!" Silver said 'pieces of eight' were gold coins, and meant good luck.

I heard someone coming, so I hid in a barrel.

One night I went to sneak an apple from the kitchen. I heard someone coming, so I hid in a barrel. It was Long John Silver and his friend, Israel Hands. They did not know that I was there. After I heard them talking, I knew that our ship was in trouble.

Chapter 4

We Declare War

Long John Silver was talking to his friend Israel Hands. "There have been some mean pirates. Some people say that Captain Bill Flint was the meanest pirate ever. But Long John Silver is the meanest pirate of all!"

Hands smiled. He looked at Silver and said, "So when do we do it? When do we kill them?" Hands was getting excited now.

Silver thought for a moment. "First we need Captain Smollett to find Treasure Island," he said. "Then we dig up the treasure.

After that, we kill the doctor, the captain, the squire, and that boy, Jim Hawkins." Silver smiled and said, "Even old Bill Flint was afraid of me."

I thought about Captain Bill Flint. He used to look out the window and worry about a pirate with one leg. Long John Silver was that pirate! Now I was worried, too.

When it was safe to leave my hiding place, I went up on the deck to find the doctor. Everyone was happy.

"Look there," he said. "It's Treasure Island!"

Captain Smollett was pointing across the water. "Look there," he said. "It's Treasure Island!"

I walked up to the doctor. I told him that we must have a meeting right away. The doctor spoke with the captain. The captain made up a story. He said that he was going to his room with the doctor, the squire, and me to celebrate our safe trip. The captain told the sailors that they could celebrate, too.

When we got to the captain's room, I told them everything that I had heard.

The squire said that Long John Silver had tricked him. The squire said that we could trust his three servants, but no one else. If Long John Silver wanted to fight, there would be 19 men on his side. There would only be six men and a boy on our side. I was the boy.

When I went out onto the deck the next morning, I felt sick. The sea was rough. Our ship was near Treasure Island and that meant that trouble would start any minute.

I hated Treasure Island and I hated myself for taking the map from Captain Flint's chest.

I looked at the island. The trees, the hills, the rocks looked gray and sad. Long John Silver said that the tallest hill was called Spy Glass Hill. It had steep sides and a flat top.

The captain had a plan. The Hispaniola was too big to get any closer to the island. The captain told Long John Silver to send all of the sailors to shore for a rest.

When the sailors heard this, they were happy. Silver told most of the sailors to get into small boats and go to the island. But Silver told Israel Hands and five other sailors to stay on the ship. Silver did not want the captain, the doctor, the squire, the servants, and me to sail away on the ship.

I decided to hide on one of the small boats and go to shore with the pirates. My boat was the first to reach the island. When I jumped out of the boat, Long John Silver saw me.

I ran deep into the thick, gray woods of the island.

He yelled for me to stop, but I kept running and running. I ran deep into the thick, gray woods of the island.

It was good to be on land again. I saw new kinds of flowers and trees. There were large flocks of birds. I sat down and felt the sun on my back. Then I heard voices. Someone was nearby! I hid among the trees and slowly crawled toward the voices. I could hear Long John Silver talking to a sailor named Tom.

"I'm sorry, Silver," said Tom. "But I will not join you and your pirates. I must obey Captain Smollett."

Just then we all heard a loud scream nearby.

"What was that?" asked Tom.

Silver laughed. "Ha, ha, ha! That's your friend Alan. He wanted to obey the captain, too!"

Tom turned and started to run. Silver grabbed his crutch and threw it at the sailor. The crutch hit Tom in the back.

Before Tom could get up, Silver stabbed him with his knife.

Tom fell, and Silver hopped over
to him. Before Tom could get up,
Silver stabbed him with his knife.

I crawled away. When it was safe,
I stood up and started to run. I ran
faster than I have ever run before.
"I can never let Silver catch me now,"
I said to myself. "If Silver catches
me, he will kill me, too. Just like
Tom and Alan."

Chapter 5

The Fighting Begins

I ran until I could not see Long John Silver. I stopped to rest. Suddenly I heard a sound on the hill in front of me. I looked and saw something running from tree to tree. Was it a bear? Was it a man? It looked dark and hairy. Now I had Silver behind me and a wild animal in front of me.

I remembered my pistol. I took out my gun, and walked slowly toward the animal. Nothing could be worse than Long John Silver.

As I got closer, I could see that
this was not an animal. It was a man.
His skin was burnt by the sun.
His lips were black. He wore bits
of rags that were held together with
string and sticks. The man got down
on his knees in front of me.

"Who are you?" I asked.

"Ben Gunn," he said. His voice was
dry and cracked. "I am poor Ben
Gunn. I have not seen another man
for three years."

"Did your ship sink in the sea?"
I asked.

"No," said Gunn. "Captain Flint
left me here to die," he said.
"But I did not die! I found Flint's
treasure. I'm rich!"

Gunn told me all about Captain
Flint. "Flint murdered six sailors
and buried their bones right here,"
he said.

I told him all about Long John
Silver. But Gunn already knew
about Silver.

Ben was afraid of Silver, too. "Silver is here," I said. "He plans to kill us all and take Flint's treasure."

Gunn said that we would fight Silver together. Gunn grabbed me by the arm and said, "Take me home, boy, and you can be rich, too!"

Gunn told me that he had made a raft and hidden it by a large white rock. He said that I could use it. Suddenly, there was an explosion. "The ship's cannon!" I said. "The fighting has begun!"

The flag was flying above an old, wooden fort.

As we walked along, Gunn saw a red, blue, and white flag. It was the flag of Great Britain! It was like the flag that Captain Smollett had on our ship!
I went slowly toward it. Was this a trick? Gunn said that it was not a trick. The flag was flying above an old, wooden fort. The fort was made of logs. Gunn said that Captain Flint had made that fort many years ago. I could see holes in the logs and guns sticking out of the holes. Smoke was rising from the fort.

I hoped that Ben Gunn was right.
I hoped that my friends were in the
fort. Gunn did not want to meet my
friends just yet. He went back into
the trees.

I got closer until I could hear voices.
It was Doctor Livesey, Squire John,
and Captain Smollett! "Hello in there!"
I called.

Doctor Livesey greeted me and
helped me into the fort. Everyone
was surprised to see me. I saw that
one of the sailors, a man named Gray,
had joined us.

Doctor Livesey greeted me and helped me into the fort.

But I also saw that one of the
squire's servants, Redruth, was
dead. "My dear old Redruth,"
said the squire. "He was shot by
one of Silver's men."

The doctor told me all the news.
They had decided to get off the
Hispaniola. They loaded up a
rowboat with guns and food and
rowed to the island. That's when
they found the fort. The pirates on
the ship had fired a cannon at them,
but missed. "I heard the cannon,"
I said.

The pirates on the ship had fired a cannon at them, but missed.

The doctor spoke again. He said
that Long John Silver and the other
pirates attacked them on the island.
The pirates had killed Redruth, but
now we were safe inside the fort.
"And now tell us about your
adventures, Jim," said the doctor.

I told them how Silver had killed
two sailors. I told them how I found
Ben Gunn. "Gunn has been here
for three years," I said. "He found
Flint's treasure." I talked and talked
until I fell asleep. But our battle with
Long John Silver was just beginning.

Chapter 6

Fighting at the Fort

The next morning, we held a meeting in the fort. Long John Silver had about fifteen pirates left. Two of them were wounded. We had seven people left at the fort: Doctor Livesey, Captain Smollett, Squire John, two of his servants, and Gray. I was the seventh.

We had enough gun powder to last a long time. But our food supply was running low. The captain said that we could beat Long John Silver if we were careful. We decided to stay in the fort and fight the pirates from there.

The wind blew sand into our fort. The sand got into our eyes. Some of the smoke from our fire went out through a hole in the roof. But most of the smoke stayed in the fort and got into our eyes, too.

We were all hard at work when someone yelled to us from outside the fort. Everyone stopped to look. It was Long John Silver and another sailor! The sailor was waving a white flag. That meant that he and Silver wanted to talk to us without fighting.

"Give us the map to the treasure," said Silver, "and we will let you live."

Silver walked right up to the fence around the fort. He threw his crutch over the fence and then climbed over!

Captain Smollett went out to see Silver. "Give us the map to the treasure," said Silver, "and we will let you live."

"Is that so?" asked the captain. "You will let us live? You can't find the treasure without the map. And you can't sail the ship without a captain."

Captain Smollett was yelling now. "If you give up, Silver, we will let you live!"

Captain Smollett was yelling now.
"If you give up, Silver, we will let
you live!"

Silver was angry. "Very well,
then! This is the last you will see
of me. Now all you will see are my
guns and bullets!" Silver grabbed
his crutch and climbed back over
the fence.

The Captain came back inside
the fort. He found us all resting.
He yelled at us. He told us to get
ready at once. He said that Silver
would be attacking soon.

In about an hour, seven pirates came running at
our fort.

We had to be ready. We loaded our guns. We put our swords on the table. We waited for the pirates to attack.

In about an hour, seven pirates came running at our fort. We all shot at them. We hit two of them and they fell to the ground. One pirate turned and ran away. But the others kept running toward the fort. Our guns were empty so we grabbed our swords and ran outside to fight the pirates. Gray stabbed one pirate in the back. The doctor cut another pirate across his neck.

The squire loaded his gun and shot
one pirate from inside the fort.
We had held them off this time!

  I went back inside the fort. One of
the squire's servants, Joyce, was
dead. Joyce had been shot through
the head. The other servant, Hunter,
lay on the floor. He was bleeding and
scared. But he was alive. Captain
Smollett had been hit in the arm.
I counted everybody that was still alive.
I told the captain that there were now
just ten pirates and six of us.

  "That's better," said the captain.

Chapter 7

My Trip on the Raft

Later that day, the Doctor went to find Ben Gunn. That left only five of us at the fort. But the squire's servant, Hunter, was dying and the captain was hurt too badly to move. That meant that only three of us, the squire, Gray, and me, would be able to fight off any pirates. And I was just a boy. When the Doctor left, I wanted to go with him. I was tired of being in that sandy, windy, and bloody fort. I wanted to be out on the island again, so I did a very bad thing.

I snuck away to find Ben Gunn's raft.

I snuck away to find Ben Gunn's raft.
Ben had told me where he had hidden
it. I wanted to find the raft, in case we
ever needed it. When Gray and Squire
John went to help the captain, I left.
It was bad of me to leave only two men
at the fort. But I just had to get out of
there for a while.

I followed Ben Gunn's directions
to his raft. It was hidden next to a big,
white rock. The raft was tiny! It was
made out of wood and goat skin.

It was hidden next to a big, white rock.

I could tell that Ben Gunn did not have any tools when he built it. I did not think that it would even float. When I saw it there, I got another idea.

Long John Silver and his pirates were still on the island. We had beaten them and I was afraid that they would give up and sail out to sea. I thought that they would leave us to die on the island. I did not want this to happen. The Hispaniola was still tied to its anchor by a long rope.

If I could float out to the ship, I could cut the rope. Then the ship would float away. Long John Silver and his men would have nowhere to go.

I got into the raft and paddled out to the Hispaniola. The raft was hard to steer. I moved slowly. When I finally got to the ship, I found the anchor rope. The rope was tight. "If I cut the rope now," I said to myself, "it might fly up and hit me." I waited for the wind to blow against the ship.

I got into the raft and paddled out to the
Hispaniola.

That would make the rope looser so that I could cut it.

While I waited for the wind, I heard voices on the ship. Long John Silver had left two pirates on the Hispaniola. They were supposed to guard it. I floated closer to the Hispaniola and peeked in at them. They were both drunk. One of them was Israel Hands. I didn't know the other one's name. He wore a red cap. He was missing all of his teeth. The sailors did not see me. They were too busy fighting with each other.

They were yelling and trying to choke
each other. I was glad that I did not
drink rum.

The wind blew against the Hispaniola.
When the anchor rope felt loose,
I cut the rope. The Hispaniola began
to float away. But the ship was pulling
my raft along with it! I thought that the
raft would tip over and I would die.
I could not see the island. There was
nothing I could do. I lay down in my
raft and held on. I thought that I would
never wake up again.

Chapter 8

Me and Hands

I did wake up, though. I woke up with the sun on my face. I looked around. I thought I would be in the middle of the ocean. But I could still see Treasure Island. My raft had been making circles around the island all night long. The waves pushed me out to sea. Then the waves pulled me back in toward the shore. Then I saw it. The Hispaniola was coming right at me! Then it stopped, turned, and went away from me. Then it came back at me again.

At first, I thought that Hands was drunk again. But even a drunk sailor could sail better than that. I decided that no one was sailing the Hispaniola. "If I could get on the Hispaniola and sail her," I said, "then I could save my friends. The pirates would be left on Treasure Island!"

I paddled toward the Hispaniola. She moved away from me. I stopped. Then the Hispaniola stopped. Then she came right at me again. I didn't have time to get out of her way.

This time the Hispaniola smashed right into my raft!

This time the Hispaniola smashed right into my raft! I jumped and grabbed onto the side of the ship. She smashed the raft into little pieces. My raft was gone and I was on the Hispaniola.

I went on board and found Israel Hands and the pirate in the red cap. Neither of them moved. They were both covered in blood. Their faces were white. "Both dead," I said. It looked like they had killed each other in their fight. Suddenly, Hands groaned.

"You're not dead, Mr. Hands?"
I said. His leg was bleeding badly.

Hands groaned again. "Jim
Hawkins," he said, "What are you
doing here?"

"Call me 'captain,'" I said.
"I'm sailing this ship now. And you
will do what I say."

"I need more rum," said Hands.
"Bring me rum and I'll do what you
say." Hands smiled an evil smile.
"Captain Jim, sir."

"First," I said, "I'm taking down your flag and putting up our flag." I pulled down the black pirate flag with its skull and crossbones. I found Captain Smollett's flag for Great Britain and put it up. I yelled to Hands. "Down with your Jolly Roger pirate flag, and up with the Union Jack flag of Great Britain!"

I went below the deck to find rum for Hands and food and water for myself. But I did not trust Hands. I snuck up another ladder and looked at him.

Hands had gotten up and found a
long, sharp knife. He hid the knife
in his shirt. Then he sat back down.

"So he wants to kill me," I said.
"Is that it?"

Below the deck, the poor Hispaniola
was a mess. The pirates had torn her
apart looking for rum and the treasure
map. I found a bottle that still had a
little rum in it. I found bread, cheese,
and fresh water. I went back on deck.
I knew that Hands would not kill me
until the ship was safe. I gave him the
rum. I wanted Hands to stay drunk.

Hands helped me sail the Hispaniola.

Hands helped me sail the Hispaniola.
I held the wheel and I did just what he
said. I steered the big ship right
around to the north end of the island.
We beached her in the sand where
she could not float away. Hands did
not like looking at O'Brien, the dead
pirate. Hands asked me to throw
O'Brien's body into the water.
I said, "No."

I was so happy with my sailing that
I forgot about Hands. He ran at me
with his knife. I saw him at the last
second and ducked.

His knife swung over my head.

I stepped back and pulled a pistol

from my belt. I pointed it at Hands

and pulled the trigger. Click!

The gun did not fire. It was wet with

sea water. Hands chased me again.

I looked around. My only choice

was to climb the rope ladder.

I climbed quickly. Hands was

climbing up, too. I re-loaded each

of my pistols. Then I aimed both

guns at Hands.

Hands reached his arm back and threw his knife at
me.

I laughed. "If you take one more step, Hands," I said, "I will blow your brains out."

Hands put his arms up. I thought he was giving up. Hands reached his arm back and threw his knife at me. Both of my guns went off. The knife stabbed me through the shoulder and pinned me to the mast. Both of my guns fell to the water far below. But so did Hands. I had killed him. The knife had cut me just a little. It had pinned my shirt and jacket to the mast. I pulled away from the knife.

I waded to shore. I was excited to tell my friends what I had done.

It was dark, but in the moonlight I could find my way. At last I found the fort. I snuck up to it and went inside. Everyone was asleep.

"I'll just lie down and surprise them in the morning," I thought. In the darkness, I kicked against something soft. A loud voice called out. It was the voice of danger!

Chapter 9

The Enemy Camp

The voice screamed, "Pieces of eight! Pieces of eight!" It was the parrot, Flint! I turned to run, but I ran right into the arms of Long John Silver. I was trapped. One of the pirates lit a torch. Now I was with six pirates, and Silver. I was sure that they had killed all my friends. Now I wished that they had killed me, too. Silver spoke into my face.

"It looks like we've got ourselves a new pirate!" he said. "You're stuck with us now. Your friends will never take you back."

Did this mean that my friends were still alive? "Where are my friends?" I asked.

"Oh, they gave up," Silver said. "They gave us the map and walked away. They were plenty mad at you, Jim Hawkins!"

I would never be a pirate. I got angry. "Silver," I said in a shaky voice. "You've lost your ship. You've lost your men. You've lost the treasure. And I am the reason for all of it."

He said he would kill any man who touched
me.

Silver looked at me. "Speak up, boy. What do you mean?" he asked.

"I'm the one who heard about your plan to kill us. I'm the one who cut the ship from its anchor. I'm the one who sailed the Hispaniola to a secret place. I am the one. The laugh is on you, Silver," I said.

The other pirates started yelling. First, they wanted to kill me. But Silver wouldn't let them. He said he would kill any man who touched me. Silver knew that I was worth more alive than dead.

Then the pirates wanted to kill Long John Silver, but they were too afraid of him.

The next morning Doctor Livesey came to the fort. Silver told him that they had found me. The doctor wanted to talk to me alone. Silver let me talk to the doctor. He walked me down to the fence where the doctor was.

"Doctor," Silver said. "I'm doing you a big favor. I'll let you talk to Jim. Then someday you can do a favor for me."

The doctor wanted to talk to me alone.

"Silver?" the doctor asked.
"You sound afraid!"

"I'm not afraid to die," Silver said.
"But I am afraid of hanging. If we
ever get back to England, don't let
them hang me!"

"If we both get off this island,"
the doctor said. "I'll remember this
favor. But until then, keep Jim close
by your side. I don't want anything
to happen to him."

Long John Silver let us talk. I told
the doctor my story.

I told him about cutting the ship free.

I told him where the ship was hidden.

I told him about Hands and O'Brien.

The doctor said that I was a hero.

He told me that he and the others

would save me.

The next morning the pirates went

looking for the treasure. Silver tied

me to him with a rope. He had guns

in both hands and one in his belt.

He told the pirates, "I'll keep Jim

with me until we find the treasure.

Then I'll make Jim here show us the

ship."

The pirate had found a skeleton.

"Then he will let the pirates kill me,"
I thought. I could not trust Silver.
I was scared.

We followed the map. We were
looking for the tallest tree on Spy
Glass hill. All of a sudden, one of
the pirates started to scream.
We all went over to him. The pirate
had found a skeleton. The bones
of the skeleton were stretched out
in a line. Long John Silver laughed.

"Those bones are pointing the way to the treasure! Old Captain Bill Flint left this skeleton as a clue!" The other pirates were not laughing. Just thinking about old Captain Flint made them scared.

Chapter 10

The Treasure

The pirates started to talk about Captain Flint. "Flint was an ugly devil," cried one of the pirates. Each pirate told a story about the mean old sea captain. They spoke softly. They thought that the dead Captain Flint might be following them. All of a sudden, we heard a voice coming from high in a tree.

The voice sang out, "Fifteen men on a dead man's chest, Yo-Ho-Ho and a bottle of rum!"

"That's Captain Flint's song!" yelled one pirate.

"It must be Flint's ghost!" said another.

The pirates wanted to run, but they were too afraid to leave Silver and me. The voice spoke again.

"Darby McGraw!" it said in a high voice. "Darby McGraw! Darby McGraw, fetch me some rum!"

"Flint said that, too," another pirate remembered. "Flint said that just before he killed old Darby."

"It's a ghost!" they all yelled. "It's a ghost!"

Silver held up his hand. The other pirates looked at him. Silver had a little smile on his face. "I know that voice," he said. "That's Ben Gunn. Flint left him here three years ago."

"Ben Gunn?" asked one pirate. "We ain't scared of no Ben Gunn, dead or alive!"

"We came all this way for treasure," said Silver. "No Ben Gunn can stop us now."

The map showed a tall tree.

They stared into a large hole where the treasure should have been.

Silver lifted his crutch and pointed
with it up the mountain. "There she
be, boys," he said.

All of the pirates ran up the hill to
the tree. When they got there, they
stopped and stared. Their mouths
were wide open. They stared into
a large hole where the treasure
should have been. But the hole was
empty! Someone else had taken the
treasure!

Silver thought fast. He knew that
the pirates would be mad at him.

He jumped to the other side of the
hole and pulled me over, too.

He handed one of his pistols to me.

There we stood. Me and Silver were
on one side of the hole. The five
pirates were on the other side.

The pirates started to come toward
us. Suddenly three gunshots rang
out: crack! crack! crack! I watched two
of the pirates fall into the hole and
die. The other three pirates ran off
down Spy Glass hill.

My friends Doctor Livesey, Gray, and
Ben Gunn stepped out from the trees.

He jumped to the other side of the hole and pulled
me over, too.

Each held a gun. They had set a trap for the pirates. Long John Silver was lucky to be with me. They would have killed him, too.

The doctor told Silver and me how his plan had worked. Ben Gunn had found the treasure two months before. He had hidden the gold in his cave. The doctor had given Captain Flint's treasure map to Silver because the treasure was already in Ben's cave. The doctor and the squire let Silver have the fort, too.

The doctor, the squire, Captain
Smollett, and Gray were all staying
in Ben Gunn's cave with the treasure.
I was happy. I had my friends, the
Hispaniola, and the treasure.

We hiked to the beach to where the
pirates had left two small rowboats.
First, the doctor used an ax to break
up one of the boats. He did not want
the three pirates to leave Treasure
Island. Then we got into the other
boat and went back to the Hispaniola.
Ben's cave was near the Hispaniola.

There was Captain Flint's treasure!

It was a large cave. Squire John was sitting near a fire and giving Captain Smollett a drink of water. I looked past the fire. There was Captain Flint's treasure! Gold coins from around the world and gold bars were piled higher than my head. We were all going to be very rich.

It took us three days to load the gold onto the Hispaniola. We did not take Captain Flint's treasure of silver. We left food and clothes and tools in Ben's cave for the three pirates. Then we sailed home.

During our trip, we stopped in South America to get more sailors and supplies. While we were there, Long John Silver stole a small boat and a bag of our gold. That was the last I have seen of the sailor with one leg.

We returned home to England. Each of us had enough gold to be rich for a lifetime. But Ben Gunn spent his share of the gold in just three weeks.

I never think about bloody Treasure Island. I never want to go back there again. In my worst dreams, I can still hear a parrot cry out, "Pieces of eight! Pieces of eight!"

The End

About the Start-to-Finish Author

John Matern grew up in northern California. He has written several short stories and novels. He also teaches in middle school and high school and he coaches little league baseball.

About the Original Author

Robert Louis Stevenson was born in Scotland in 1850 and died in 1894. He fought against sickness and poor health throughout his short life. His weak lungs forced him to travel to places where the air was warm and pure. Out of these travels came two great adventure stories, *Treasure Island* and *Kidnapped* — you can find both of these stories in the Start-to-Finish library.